Published by Blurb for Ecaabooks
https://au.blurb.com/user/Ecaabooks

Copyright © Ecaabooks

Copyright © text and design: Jacquelyn Nicholson

Copyright © images: Jacquelyn

All rights reserved. Without limiting the rights above, no part of this publication maybe reproduced or transmitted, in any form or by any means (electronic, mechanical, photocopying, recording or otherwise) without the prior written permission of both the copyright owner and the above publisher of this book.

© 2019 by Ecaabooks, and the author of this book. The book author retains sole copyright to her contributions to this book.

Introduction

Sharks are unique creatures and have been around for a long time, swimming the oceans for 400 million years, they have survived mass extinction events, the sea is their domain! An unusual marine habitat which is a substantial volume of water. From deep trenches to the shallows of the shoreline sharks have continuously roamed. This is not surprising when the ocean takes up more than 70 per cent of all the surface of the earth. The shark's sensory system is so finely tuned that they are remarkably adapted to their surroundings making them an acute highly skilled hunter and they can hunt alone or with other sharks.

Humans are not so streamlined and are more clumsy in the water, we wobble along as we swim and tend to be the complete opposite to these fast moving fish. We're taught one has more chance of being hit by a car than being attacked by a shark. The odds of having a shark attack you or even kill you are approx 3,748,000 to 1. So you would have to be the unluckiest person in the world. It is a bit like winning the lotto but on the other end of the scale unless you live in some places like Western Australia where the odds can be far different to the rest of the world (for swimming and surfing, it has been approx. 1 in 40,000, and for divers, its been 1 in 16,000).

Australia is surrounded by water on all sides, most of the Australian people live along the coast as the interior is mostly just dessert and the northern parts of Australia from Broome in the west to Rockhampton in the east have the added dangers of the saltwater crocodiles. Swimming and surfing is a national past time, and when sharks and humans are in the same place at the same time, sometimes it can be quite a balancing act.

When the words Shark Attack is mentioned, the first thing which comes across people's minds are Man-eaters, the Great White Shark! But in general, sharks don't go out of their way to attack humans. And it's not always a great white shark that has attacked someone. However many shark attacks have very little or nothing in common apart from the fact that humans and sharks were at the same place, at the same time.

No matter when these encounters with sharks happen, sometimes unprovoked attacks occur and they generally don't turn out well.

Contents

Copyright	2
Introduction	3
Contents	5
Fatal V Survival	6
Helpful Hints	8
True Stories	10
Grey Nurse Shark	40
Bull Shark	41
Man V Shark	42
Surviving a shark attack	44
Great White Shark	47

Fatal V Survival

Generally, we only hear about shark attacks when there has been some loss of limb or even death, but shark attacks happen more frequently than we really realize. Most times its just being in the wrong place at the wrong time, dive bombing them from a boat, jetty or they feel some threat from someone which can cause an attack. Sometimes it can come down to how you behave in the water and or if the shark was hungry or just wanted to investigate the area where you were swimming / diving. Other times it's in locations where there has been previous attacks or significant loss of life, like a shipwreck or some disaster event and they remember. Like tapping on a fish tank's glass, the sound wave is vibrated through the water and the fish react, turning quickly or darting away scared of the noise. The sound waves we make in the sea, can sound like fun to us, but to the marine life under the water, it could sound like some possible doom or attraction. As humans we don't tend to think about what is going on around us so much or how this or that is going to effect some other creature that we all really don't understand.

But in reality, swimming and surfing are just like going jogging in a wildlife park where the animals roam free, sooner or later encounters with sharks are inevitable. Most of these encounters are harmless, but some are more traumatic or even fatal.

People say, sharks only attack by mistake or accidental; they can't see you, they don't mean it! But some like the Great White shark are very intelligent; they have to be smarter than the prey they are hunting, like dolphins and seals the shark has to be able to outwit its prey, or it is going to go hungry. Dolphins are highly intelligent mammals, and if a shark is going to have one for lunch, it has to be smarter than the average dolphin to catch one.

When a shark comes in for an exploratory bite, they are sampling what is on the dinner table which would be the case if they only took one bit and left, but that's not always right.
At what point does it become intentional; an attack is it when they come back for a second or third bite. When is it no longer an exploratory exercise, is it when a shark has taken a person under the water, and that person is fighting for their life; against a strong willing fish. When a shark is shaking you violently underwater, it is no longer exploring, it is trying to eat you for lunch or dinner.

But no matter the reason for a shark attack, it comes down to one main factor... If your not Shark, your bait! A food source. It doesn't matter how you want to slice and dice it, we go into their home and we are no longer in control.

Slow swimming land mammals like us, won't stand a chance against any fast-moving killing machine, so we have to change the possible outcome in the first place.

Helpful hints for surviving a shark attack

The prospect of surviving a shark attack can be significantly improved when people follow a few precautions to reduce the likelihood before entering the water.

It is best to avoid swimming or surfing during dawn, dusk & night when sharks are most active - hunting at these known periods.

Its strongly recommended that people swim and surf at patrolled beaches only, where surf lifesavers can keep a watchful eye while you have fun in the water.

Avoid swimming after substantial periods of rain in polluted waterways or at river mouths or estuaries.

Watch out for large schools of fish, mainly bait-fish, because sharks like to feed on them.

Watch out for birds, dive bombing for fish, as this could be lots of bait-fish, which will attract sharks.

Don't wear shiny jewelery into the water, or you could be mistaken for a pretty tasty fish with shiny scales.

Don't swim in blackish dirty water; this gives the shark the perfect opportunity to watch you without you knowing.

Don't go into the water if you have any cuts and scratches that are bleeding. Sharks can smell a drop of blood from miles away!

Don't wear bright colored swim wear or clothes when in the water as sharks in general, are attracted to these colors, especially great whites react to reds and yellows. Wear bland natural colors like blues and browns, not white or skin tones.

If diving from a boat or jetty always check the water first to make sure it is safe to do so, Sharks can react to the sounds of you hitting the water.

Don't swim out too far, stay close to the shore, remember if a shark does come, you don't want to be the one person in the water trying to get back to the beach, sharks can spot their prey from 70 to 100 feet away.

One has to think, wisely when buying beachwear; that red and yellow swimsuit may looking stunning on you, the sharks will certainly think so.

Swim in groups, just like a school of fish, the healthy ones swim together and sick injured fish swim along alone.

Have less salt content in your body before going for a swim at the beach. Salt water contains sodium and chlorine **ions**. these Ions particles have an electrical charge because they have lost or gained an electron. Sharks can sense someone more easily if you have more salt in their body.

Shark Attack

These stories are real, they happened to someone, some more shocking than others, But they all have one thing in common, a shark. These people were carrying out their normal daily lives, and by remembering their struggle, in some small way, we honor them.

Saturday the 23rd of February 1935, a young boy aged six years, had to be rescued after being swept out into the breaking surf near Manly, Sydney, New South Wales; he was swimming at the South Steyne Beach when the incident occurred.
The boy was seen out in the breakers when a shark, was noticed in the channel six yards from the shore, and the shark alarm was sounded. Lifesavers had to swim across the channel to reach the boy, while the 10-foot shark was cruising. A doctor was preparing for any eventualities that could arise from this rescue. The boy recovered after treatment and the shark after traveling along the beach for half an hour just disappeared.

++++

It was reported in a local paper Saturday 1st March 1975, on Friday a group of eight surfers were paddling on their boards off Cotters Lake Beach, Wilsons Promontory, Victoria, Australia. When a group of sharks were swimming near the surfers, Mr Bassett, 22 years of Yanakie was attacked by one of the sharks and is recovering in hospital with 75 stitches to his leg.

++++

A 12-foot shark was sighted about 200 yards off the Port Lincoln town Jetty this morning, the 25th of February 1953, where most people swim and the crew of a boat said the shark was near by.

In front of hundreds of surfers on the Sunday afternoon, the 7th January 1934, Colin Grant aged 22 years, a former surf and belt champion of the club, was in about 5-foot of water waiting for a wave at Queenscliff Beach when a shark attacked him. In the unprovoked attack, the shark inflicted terrible injuries to his leg, stripping the flesh from the knee down to practically only the bones were remaining. When Les Grant, the son of Sgt. Grant of the Manly Police station and no relation to the victim saw Colin in trouble, he put the belt on and waded out to Collins. Les lifted Colin out of the water with the assistance of K. Parkhill and a tourniquet was applied by the Queenscliff club member, Mr P. J. Smith.

He was rushed by ambulance, to the Manly hospital where Mr Grant underwent an operation this afternoon to remove a portion of his leg, due to gangrene developing. The Doctors at the hospital said Colin was suffering from so much loss of blood and shock that his condition was noted as critical, but are hopeful to save his life. The president of the club, Mr Thomas Boatwright, was selected from many volunteers to give blood for the transfusion and is resting in bed. Meanwhile the club is raising money for the Colin Grant Fund.

++++

A shark siren was sounded at Glenelg, South Australia on Friday the 28th of November 1947, when two 10-foot sharks were sighted off the Glenelg Jetty late in the afternoon. The sharks remained for some time swimming around the end of the jetty before swimming out to sea.

shark Attack   True Stories

Leon Hermes, aged approx 15 years was attacked at North Steyne beach, so severely injured by the shark attack, that he died shortly afterwards on the first Sunday of April 1934. The shark came at him three times biting at the flesh on his leg. He was the honoring junior champion of the North Steyne Surf Lifesaving Club as he was too young to join yet, and he often went swimming after attending the Manly church service on Sunday mornings. On this occasion at about mid-day, he and his friend George Herd, aged 17, entered the water and were swimming 80 yards from shore, well out in the breaking surf and there was about ten yards between the two friends.
The attack occurred suddenly, and Leon uttered a cry and yelled out " For God's sake SHARK", the water immediately changed to crimson color and Leon called out for help. As the shark could not been seen George, heard Leon's cry for help over the noise of the crashing breakers and went at once to his friend's assistance.

As George was trying to get Leon to shore he noticed his friend had been terribly mutilated along his leg, at Leon's thigh, knee and ankle and blood was gushing out causing a stream like effect in the water. A bank manager from Mandurama, who was holidaying at Manly for some time, a Mr Horniman who was on a closer to shore set of breakers, swam over to help Herd, where he could. Upon hearing Herd's call for help, three members from the North Steyne club rushed into the water to assist in the rescue.

Colin Grant had witnessed the attack on Leon from the shore as he was sitting on the beach preparing to go into the water,

Leon was carried ashore in a complete state of collapse; first aid was rendered to try to stop the flow of blood from escaping and he was rushed to the Manly District Hospital but died soon afterwards from the great loss of blood. Leon was a scholar of fine character with a promising bright future ahead of him, he was born in Adelaide, South Australia and the family moved
sometime later to the Manly area of New South Wales.
A Constable from Broken Hill, who was visiting Manly, Mr Wise, saw the shark come close to shore a quarter of an hour after Leon had been taken out of the water. He thought it was a Grey Nurse variety about 14 ft long and it was cruising along the shoreline.
He grabbed a oar and without thinking ran into the water to hit it, but backed off when a boy had thrown a rock at it and the shark just turned rapidly, heading down along the beach parallel to the shore.
George Herd was a member of the club, and he was quite modest over his part in rescuing his friend because of any further probable attacks.
The Coroner, Mr Farrington, congratulated George Herd for his actions, who had forgotten the dangers to himself and gone to assist his friend.

++++

Six surfers at North Narrabeen were warned by people on the beach, that there were sharks between them and the shore. As the surfers made for the shoreline the sharks swam out and passed within 25 yards of them.

++++

True Stories

Ray Land, lost his life during a shocking shark attacked at Bar Beach near Newcastle, on the New South Wales coastline of Australia, during a weekend Surf lifesaving event in January 1949. The young man was attacked in seven foot of water, by a 14 foot (4.26 meter) shark. The shark threw Land, in a backward somersault and dragged him to the bottom, where Land fought the shark under the water, his hands were torn and he was missing two fingers on his right hand. Ray, 20 years old, was the Northern District Senior Surf Champion and was competing in the A division, of the fourth heat of the Rescue and Resuscitation championships.

In this heat the six-member teams drew positions from a bag, containing six marbles, then each member lines up in their chosen position behind the reel, Ray pulled out the belt man marble, which was position no. 2. His line fouled on the beach shortly after the race had started when he had only gotten about ten yards, which held him up for only a few seconds. Ray's patient, Mr Mckie, had made it to the buoy in second place while Ray and the other two team's, belt-men were swept slightly northward while swimming out to their patients. Only a few yards had separated the three teams when Ray's line got snared around a rock about 100 yards out from the shore and he signalled for assistance, by swinging his right arm across his head and when Reg Gazzard, another team member of Ray's team, saw Ray waving his arm, he left the beach to swim out towards him. Mckie also saw Ray waving his arm and swam towards Ray from the buoy, while Trew came in from behind the buoys, to stand by on his surf ski. The patrolling boat was told to go over near Ray by the loudspeaker on the shore and as the boat got near to Ray, they gave the raised oars signal for a shark and then the siren was sounded. Shortly afterwards a large wave broke over the rocks and Ray was pulled under by the shark, then a large pool of blood could be seen spread through the foaming and unbroken water.

The shark had struck Ray only once inflicting terrible wounds to Ray's left leg. It gashed his calf open and his leg was almost severed at his thigh. Trew, a member of the Cook's Hill Surf Club got to Ray just as he was coming up to the surface and dragged him across the surf ski he was on. Once the siren sounded, Gazzard turned around and caught a wave back to the beach, while Mckie swam to the boat, which had already picked up the other team's belt-men and Noel Long the (Merewether patient) and Bob Carlon (Cooks Hill patient).

Trew said he saw Ray's signal, so he went in to stand by. He was about 10 yards away when he saw something in the water. Trew first thought he had seen a dolphin, but then he saw Ray disappear under the water and a large patch of blood appeared. When Ray came up, Trew said he saw Ray and he was kicking and fighting with the shark with his hands. Then the shark let him go and Trew dragged Ray on to his surf ski. Another big wave washed over both of them and overturned the surf ski, the shark was right under them. Trew again managed to drag Ray on to the ski and then headed towards the boat. Baker and Campbell, of Cooks Hill Club, rang for an ambulance when the alarm had been given. Other members and officials had gathered dry towels from spectators and had them ready with the stretcher and the shark emergency kit on the beach. A line was set up just in case the boat bringing Ray in overturned in the surf. He was transferred to the ambulance on the stretcher and taken to the hospital.

Where his parents met him, after watching the shark attack unfold from the beach.

A call over the loudspeakers for members to give blood and a truck took 12 members to the Newcastle Hospital a few minutes later. Ray died in the hospital a quarter of an hour later.

++++

Ron Johnson, a young youth of only 16 years and a milk carter, was fatally mauled by a 12 ft (3.65 meters) shark on Thursday morning, late in the month of February 1948. Ron suffered terrible injuries to the right leg and thigh, so much so that the muscles on the calf of the leg had been ripped away.

Ron was a junior member of the Stockton Surf Club and had only been in the water for about half an hour with seven other members from the club. His friends, that were with him caught a good size set of waves to the shore, which left Ron alone, waiting for the next set to come.

The beach inspector, Mr Harry Stephenson, who was in the shark tower, had just finished calling out to Ron's companions. " Hey, there is your mate out there" when the shark struck without warning, Ron was about 40 yards from shore in six foot of water, still close enough for the spectator's on the beach to hear the youth screaming in pain and then see blood spread rapidly over the water.

Mr Stephenson said, I had glanced over towards where Johnson was swimming and then I saw what appeared to be a tail and dorsal fin of a shark, Johnson then started screaming and shouted out "A SHARK HAS GOT ME". I saw a pattern of blood on the water and Johnson was trying to swim to shore and I Shouted out "SHARK!" At that moment I saw Albert Linich, a club member, ran out of the Pavilion and straight down to put the belt on, as I was scrambling down from my tower. Linich rushed straight out into the water and headed for Johnson. "It was the bravest thing I have ever seen."

Linich continued to wade out to reach Johnson, who was still conscious at the time. He picked Johnson up in his arms and brought him back to the beach.

"Stokes, another club member, Linich and myself was carrying Johnson to the ambulance room when we were met by Dr Walker, of Stockton." said Stephenson. Johnson's blood was pouring out from terrific injuries to his thigh and lower legs. Johnson gasped out "I never had a chance"

Dr Walker administered oxygen, but Johnson had suffered such loss of blood that he lost consciousness and died shortly afterwards.

++++

January 24th 1954, 35 miles from Thursday Island, Mrs Mills 30 years old, was spearfishing with her husband when a five-foot shark attacked her and she sustained a badly lacerated arm. She was rushed to the hospital and recovering.

Shark Attack

A terrible accident occurred on Sunday the 23rd of December 1934, while 14 years old, Roy Inman was swimming with his sister at Woy Woy, near Horsfield Bay, north of Sydney, New South Wales. The family was holidaying at a boathouse on the bay. Roy and his sister, Joyce, aged 12 years, entered the water from the back of the boathouse shortly after 1 pm. The water at this part was about 12 foot deep.
Roy had been swimming around for some time and Joyce was swimming closer to the shore which was only about four foot away. When Roy had decided to climbed onto the slipway, which was used for launching a boat and went over to the jetty and dived into the water. As the shark immediately was making its attack, it brushed against Joyce as it swam past, who was, panic-stricken with fear and quickly made her way to the shore. A few seconds later she turned around to see the shark attacking her brother, as the shark had practically thrown him from the water and turned him over. Roy was screaming and tried frantically to reach the jetty but the shark attacked again and dragged him beneath the blood-stained water and disappeared.
Mr Herbert Inman, the father of Roy and Joyce, said he was working at the back of his week-ender when he heard his 20 year old daughter screaming out "SHARK, SHARK!" After he had raced down to the front, Kathleen was already rowing in a boat near the end of the jetty.
Kathleen, later stated that she saw a very large shark which appeared to be swimming in the direction of Joyce. When she heard Joyce screaming and the discolored water, she thought

the worst, that Joyce had been attacked, but the shark's fin, however, had only grazed her as the shark was dashing towards her brother.

Roy had performed a double somersault from what appeared to be the edge of the jetty and had just risen to the surface when he immediately disappeared again. That was when Kathleen realized the shark was attacking her brother.

Kathleen, quickly thinking, jumped into a rowing boat and she began to row out to give her brother assistance when she saw Roy come up to the surface all covered in blood. She rowed frantically to reach the spot where she last saw him, but he had disappeared. She saw the shark, which then was under her boat and it almost immediately swam back into the mainstream of the bay and disappeared.

Mr Inman said, his daughters and other son had been swimming close to the jetty all morning and his other daughter was about to go back into the water when the tragedy occurred.

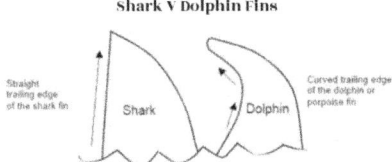

Junior members of the Maroubra Surf Club sighted the tail and a fin of a shark at 11 am, there was a rush for safety. The shark was about 8-foot long and was about seven yards from swimmers when first seen.

++++

Shark Attacks

An unusual escape from a shark happened Tuesday 9th of April 1918 at Berry's Point, Sydney Harbor when a man named Ansell, a fireman from a steamship in the port jumped overboard in a complete panic state.

The man was traveling on a steamer from Parramatta to the port when he thought he was hearing men chase him, he walked to the edge of the deck of the steamship and leaped into the water from the side of the boat. No sooner had he came back up to the surface of the water that a shark estimated at 13 foot in length headed straight for him. The people on the steamship saw the shark and started to call out to the man, who was unaware of the danger he had just placed himself in until the shark was just about to attack. The man started splashing madly about, which seemed to scare the shark away, and it disappeared for a time. Later the shark returned to attack again, but the man had been rescued back into the boat, he was not injured, but the ordeal shook the man to his core. Later he was taken to the police station to be admitted for treatment.

++++

As of the 28th December 1965, most attacks had occurred north of the Tropic of Capricorn during all months, and south of the Tropics mainly between November and April, with January being the peak season. Times of attacks ranged from 5 am to 8 pm, but a sample of 64 attacks had shown 40 between 3 and 6 pm.

A fisherman named Cox, near Port Arlington, Victoria, Australia had an unfortunate incident with a shark on Wednesday 1st of November 1899, when the monster savagely attacked his vessel and tried to eat his boat. The shark seized the keel and shook the small sailing vessel violently with such force, causing one of the gunwales underwater.

Moments later the shark was trying to break through the bottom of the boat, crunching on the wooden boards of the hull. The shark then returned for another attacked and charged at the vessel from the stern but missed its mark and shot its head about 2 foot over the bow. Cox quickly pulled up the anchor and sailed off, away from that area.

Cox Reached the shore without further incident. After an examination of the vessel, it was found that the shark's jaw was at least 2 foot across with an opening of about 20 inches. A tooth from the shark had become lodged between the wooden planks of the hull, and it measured approx 2 inches tall.

++++

On Wednesday the 17th August 1949, a shark attacked and severely mauled Bob Kay aged 18 years in shallow water near Flinders Island late in the afternoon.

Bob was taken to the Yarram Hospital, where his condition was reported as severe. He was on a fishing trip with the ketch Surprise, from Port Welshpool, Victoria and went swimming. He had been in the water only a few minutes when he was attacked. The other members of the party beat off the shark and rushed Mr Kay to the hospital.

True Stories

On the 6th December 1951, a tragic shark attack occurred at the Merewether Beach, near Newcastle, New South Wales. When Frank Okulick aged 21 years, and an Australian Surf-ski Champion was out swimming with fellow club members, Bill Morgan aged 24, John Blackett 30, and James Robert Johns 25, the three lifesavers had seconds before the attack, caught a wave to the shore.

An 8-foot shark savagely attacked the boy, again and again, dragging him approx 100 yards from the shore. A man who claimed had seen a dark shadow in a crest of the giant wave near the youth when he had missed the previous wave set with his friends, and the man said it looked like it was bigger than a man as the shark tugged the youth under suddenly. When Frank came up, he was madly waving his arms while screaming in pain; the shark kept going back attacking him, over and over again until his head just bobbed up and down like a cork in the waves and the water was stained with his blood. After a little while, I saw the shark have another go at him, and then he disappeared, said the man. Meanwhile, Morgan who had reached the shore, along with Ron Galbraith aged 23, also a lifesaver from the club went out with two surf ski's, but by the time they had reached the approx spot, franks body had disappeared. News of the attack traveled to other clubs along the beaches, and once lifesavers at Newcastle Beach had heard about the incident, they crewed a surf boat and traveled the 2 miles to reach the Merewether Beach to give any assists possible. Not long after the attack the beach inspectors closed the beach and sounded the shark alarm.

A little after 4 pm, an hour after Frank Okulick's body had disappeared, a youth was sitting on rocks near the middle of the beach when they noticed the body in the shallow waters and started pointing at the spot. Robert Mather, a Merewether lifesaver, rushed into the water, to the spot in the surf to recover Franks mutilated remains. The shark had violently mauled him on every part of his body except for his head.

Frank had been living with his widowed mother, and He had won numerous lifesaving competitions during that year including the Australian singles surf ski championships in Western Australia. Only just recently in November Frank had won the ski championships at the North Stockton Carnival, where he and another fellow club mate, McIntosh helped in rescuing a surf boat when they swam 300 yards out with lines when the surf-boat had capsized.

++++

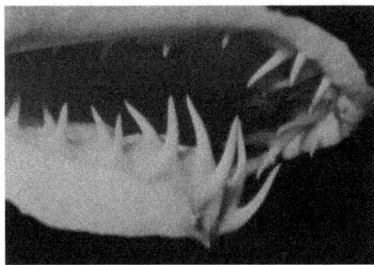

At Newport six sharks were seen cruising 100 yards offshore about mid-day. The shark bell was sounded and 60 bathers rushed from the water.

++++

While bathing in the Lane Cove River, near Chatswood, Sydney, New South Wales at roughly 6 pm on Saturday the 10th of January 1903, a young man, named Stanley James aged 20 years had his leg torn off by a shark, just above the knee. The young lad had gone to bath with his two younger brothers, and he left them both in shallow water, while he waded a little further into the river.

The river was half fresh and half salt water, and although sharks had been seen quite some way up the river, this section was thought to be a safe spot for bathing. Suddenly Stanley heard a splash near him as if a large dog had jumped into the water. Alarmed Stanley started to swim back to the shallows when he felt a terrible pain of something sharp cutting into his leg as the shark was biting down with a terrible force. James was struggling desperately for his life, trying to withstand the monster's attack, while attempting to drive it off. The young man was dragged, below the surface, but he kept fighting the shark until he managed to get away. James then started to swim to the shore while yelling drastically for help while a boat had come into view. When Mr Marsh and some ladies heard the young man screaming out for some assistance, they quickened their speed at once. Just after Mr Marsh's boat had picked up the pace, the shark made another furious rush on the lad and attacked him again, but as it gripped his leg the force of the jaws broke the bones and the leg was torn off in a sudden violent act. Afterwards, the shark disappeared beneath the blood-stained water.

After assisting his mate James to the shore, Mr Marsh improvised a tourniquet made from ladies silk handkerchiefs to stop the bleeding, The young sufferer who was conscious several times had expressed pleasure of how he fought the monster away.

Meanwhile, another boat with a group of men arrived, consisting of Messrs T. Cook, J. F. Walker, J. Bentley, W. Bear, A. J. Hogan and A. Haynes, they wrenched a door off the hinges from a nearby boat-shed and used it as a stretcher to move the young victim over rocks and through the scrub to his home.

Dr Crabbe was visiting Stanley's home at the time, so he attended to Stanley until the local ambulance brigade, under the Executive officer Holt, arrived soon after to convey him to the hospital. When, Stanley's pulse became so low on the way to the hospital they had to stop at Dr Milnes residence in Berry-street, North Sydney, where restoratives were applied. Stanley who was conscious the most of the time and had been chatting freely with those around him, died at 9:45 pm in the presence of his stepfather, Dr Milne and the ambulance officers. Both Mr Marsh and Stanley James were members of the Civil Ambulance Brigade.

++++

Portion of a trunk of a tree about 10-foot long and a big girth was mistaken for a shark by bathers at Bondi.

During an enjoyable day at Cronulla, Sydney, New South Wales, a boy staggered up a beach after feeling some pain in his leg and spoke to a lifesaver on duty, "Something bumped into me."

Ian Nolan had gone to the Cronulla beach with his family, and he had been swimming in the surf when he felt a hefty bump on his leg. When Ian was in the accident room, he said " I couldn't see the shark, but there was a lot of thrashing going on around me in the water. I didn't know I had been bitten until I got to the beach and saw blood running down my leg." After the lifesavers who examined the injuries on Ian's thigh said, there were clear signs of teeth, bite marks on his leg from a reasonably large shark, and his stomach just had a few scratches. After treatment he was allowed to be taken home to rest.

++++

News had reached Port Moresby during January 1954 of an incident of a native, aged 26 years old had survived an attack from a 14-foot shark.

The native was swimming at Singour, some 60 miles from Madang when the shark attacked him from behind. The man screamed out in pain, and shouts from his friends scared the beast away after the first attack, which gave his friends enough time to remove him from the water and placed him in a canoe, he then was taken to the Saidor outpost. The imprints of the shark's teeth extended in a circular shape from the middle of his back to down to his thigh and in some places were two inches deep. He was taken by plane to Madang where his condition was satisfactory.

A professional fisherman survived a violent attack on his small dingy, by a shark during November 1951 off the Mackay coast, Queensland.

He was working alone on an uncharted reef near the outer edge of the Barrier Reef about 90 miles northeast of Mackay. He had been getting good strikes with the Turrum and Trout, despite the presence of about 12 Blue Pointer and Grey Nurse sharks in the vicinity. As he had been gutting a Turrum, he noticed the sharks had left, and he couldn't see any more fish around in the clear water under his boat.

In the next instant, a giant Hammerhead shark struck the side of the boat reasonably hard, where the blood had been seeping through the drain hole in the cockpit floor.

The fisherman bashed the surface of the water with a heavy oar to frighten the shark off, but it attacked again leaving teeth scares on the bottom of the boat. In fear of a more violent attack on his dingy, the fisherman zig-zagged his boat towards shallow water with the 15-foot shark following the trail from 5 to 30 foot behind the boat into water only about 3 feet deep and the shark's dorsal fin at that point was standing out about 18 inches tall. The fisherman finally lost the shark by circling round in different directions, and he headed off to another location.

++++

Two members of the Freshwater Surfing Club narrowly escaped an 8-foot shark. They managed to get on top of a wave which carried them ashore.

Shark Attack

Late in the day on Monday the 31st of December 1934 a terrible accident occurred when a young man, aged 19 years, had been racing his two companions across the Georges River at Milperra, near Sydney. Richard George Foden, who lived with his foster parents in Canberra, along with the two companions, his foster brother Peter Lawrence and Ernest Edwards entered the water at 4:30 pm they were swimming across the 50 yard river to get to the other side. Richard quickly took the lead and when he was about thirty yards across a shark seized him, ripping his leg open. He shouted at the other two as the shark attacked, although shockingly mauled Richard swam on towards the shore after freeing himself from the shark's gripping teeth. The flesh ripped and torn on his right leg, from the knee to the thigh.
Meanwhile, onlookers waded into the water to reach the boy. As a fisherman grabbed him to carry him ashore, he died in the man's arms. Some of his rescuers couldn't believe he died, so they took him to shore and tore up their shirts to try bandaging his cuts. But he lost a tremendous amount of blood from the injuries inflicted on him, everyone was amazed how he managed to swim ashore. The body was sent across the river in a rowing boat and taken to hospital where life was formally pronounced dead. The shark was thought to be a Grey-nurse about 12-foot and had been seen earlier during the day by some fishermen. George Markham, a fisherman who witnessed the attack said "I saw the black fin of a shark just a few yards away from him. I was powerless to move as I saw the shark turn and rush at the young man; the water immediately turned red. I grabbed him, and his hand suddenly went limp in mine. I carried him out of the water,

but he died in my arms." Shortly afterwards and only 3 miles up the river just after 8 pm Mrs Morrin, took her five young children down to the George River, at Kentucky, Sydney for a swim to cool off. The family sat on the shore and rested for some time until a man named James Schofield arrived and the children decided to enter the water together.

The river gradually dropped away out towards the middle where the channel flowed faster; the whole river is only about a hundred yards across here. The children waded out close to the shore; they were playing, laughing and splashing each other while their mother was sitting on the bank watching them.

Beryl, aged 13 years, along with her brother aged ten years and slightly behind her, swam out about 10 yards from the shore to a sandbar in the stream where the water is about four foot deep. Suddenly; Beryl started screaming in terrible agony, and a violent splashing noise was heard from the shore. Thomas thought she was joking around and told the others not to take notice of her until Beryl kept persisting in her agonizing screaming and Mrs Morrin asked the man to go find out what was the matter with her. As James waded in and swam out to the bank, Beryl, still screaming and moaning pitifully she lifted the mangled stumps of her arms saying "A SHARK has got me, my arms are gone." James; was horrified to see the nature of her injuries. Her arm had been torn right off above her elbow, and her left hand had been bitten through and only hanging on by a piece of flesh. James quickly grabbed her arms above the elbows and exerted an enormous pressure to stop the blood from gushing out from her wounds as Beryl was almost at the point of collapse and he carried her towards the shore when Mrs Young, who lived nearby, and heard her screams jumped straight into the water fully clothed to assist him half way. Meanwhile, the other terror-stricken children scrambled ashore crying and watched in horror as their older sister was placed on the shoreline. Ligatures were hastily applied from towels and belts to help stop the gushing of blood. One of the children rushed to the nearby public telephone for the ambulance to come at once. On the way, officers stopped to pick up Dr Thomson, and they raced to the scene. The little girl got immediate treatment and pain relief for her terrible injuries. The ambulance rushed her to the Canterbury District Hospital where they operated on her at once; unfortunately, they found it was necessary to amputate her left arm below her elbow. With so much blood loss, they say she's in a critical condition, during the night the doctors and nurses said they would wait and see if she would survive. News of the attack on a little girl quickly spread through the neighborhood, and the fisherman went out last night setting baited hooks to catch the monster. Beryl survived her ordeal, during the coming weeks and months, fund raising events began to raise money for her, and by July she was writing letters to thank people, with the stumps of her arms.

++++

Tipped off a surf ski by a huge shark at Cronulla today, Ernest Baker, a member of the Cronulla Surf Life Saving Club, managed to reach the shore uninjured. The shark snapped at him twice but missed.

William Dobson was aged 33 years, single and resided in Petersham, a small suburb of Sydney, New South Wales where he worked as an ironmonger. He had been bathing in the Georges River, some 30 miles from the mouth of the river, when he was attacked and died almost immediately upon reaching the shore from his horrific injuries.

William and his brother John were members of a grand picnic party on Sunday afternoon in January 1906. The picnic was intended to be held, near the town of Como, an outer suburb of Sydney, but they couldn't find a lovely enough spot, so instead after the train boats, had been arranged, they traveled two or three miles further up the river past the bridge and arriving at a landing near the place called The Moons. The day had been a grand fanfare, and as it was a reasonably hot day, William Dobson announced his intentions of going for a swim to cool off, he left the picnic party along with his brother John and another picnicker and they proceeded a little further up the river. Of the three of them, only William decided to go into the water while the others sat on the bank waiting under a big shady gumtree chatting to each other.

No sooner had William dived in and swam about five yards when his companions were startled by hearing William screaming in agony and crying out loud "Oh my!! help me please, Oh my God! Get off you horrible brute, help me". They ran to the water's edge where they saw a tremendous amount of splashing going on around John's brother and through the rising spray in the air, William was frantically bashing something close to him while in constant screams of pain and making sad groaning sounds. Then his companions saw a large fin raising out of the water, rushing in, again and again, they suddenly realized it was a shark, attacking him.

William was making a gallant fight for his life, and the fish pulled him under several times, but he kept struggled madly to break free.

As the two men reached him, he managed to get away from the monstrous shark, and he fell at their feet in a semiconscious state. The two men lent down in a hurried state and quickly picked up their fallen friend and carried him to the bank where they gazed at his horrible injuries in shock. His right hand was missing entirely, and a big piece of his flesh had been torn away revealing his internal organs. His feet were shockingly lacerated while blood was streaming from every tooth gash all over his body. Poor William, didn't stand a chance and only survived a few minutes after reaching the bank.

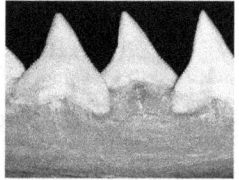

Police believe that Harold Kenneth Sterne, 53, who has been missing since early on Tuesday, may have been taken by a shark in an attempt to swim to Magnetic Island from Kissing Point.

++++

Sunday the 21st December 1952 two fishermen had survived a savage attack by an 8-foot shark in shallow waters near Cape Douglas, on the South Coast of South Australia.

John Holmes, was sent to the Mount Gambier hospital with severe gashes on his back where the shark bit him, but his condition is reported to be satisfactory.

Holmes and William McIntyre were in waist deep water setting a net. The shark bumped Holmes then returned and attacked him. It then made a run at McIntyre, it went between his legs and lifted him clear out of the water, he weighed fifteen stone.

++++

Miss Emma Pickering, a sculler, had an exciting experience when in Sydney on Tuesday, 10th January 1914. While she was pulling in an outrigger on the George's River during the morning, a 16-foot long shark attacked the frail craft, charging right into it which caused it to rock perilously.

Emma dashed straight for the shore with the shark in hot pursuit and she reached the land safely.

The shark then turned to attack her brother's boat, but he also reached the shore without any mishap.

++++

A 9-foot. shark was caught near Broome and when cut open it had a human arm inside. The arm belonged to Kathleen Mary Passaris (22) of West Perth, who was attacked by a shark in 5 feet of water.

++++

True Stories

Valma Tegal aged 14 years, and a second-year student at St. Georges High School was killed while swimming in about three foot of water at Oatley Bay, George's River on Saturday 5th of January 1946 by an 8-foot shark.

She was very popular, and a keen student who had a love for music.

Valma had been swimming and diving off a small old pier with her father, Rudolph Tegel and her cousin, Barbara Walters aged 13 years, at a small beach near their home for about 25 minutes.

A few minutes later, Valma cried out, "Dad!, Help me, come here quickly!"

Her father rushed over to her to see what was wrong, and as he reached her, she fell over as the shark had taken her left leg and severely mauled the other.

He caught her with his right arm, and she said, "Dad!, my leg's gone." He saw blood in the water and found that the shark was between his legs.

When Mr Tegel beat and kicked the shark and it swam away. Mr Tegel, said: "Valma was killed within 60 feet of her bedroom. My daughter did not have a chance. The shark gave no indication of his presence, and the water was calm, without a ripple, while this shark made his attack."

"After the attack. I lifted Valma in my arms and waded ashore with her. She died in my arms as I placed her on the sand."

"Who knows why I have lost my daughter, and I hope my loss will be a lesson to others who might lose their lives bathing in these waters. We have been living at Oatley for two years, and the only time I have seen a shark where we were swimming was seven months ago."

"People living on the foreshore usually swim from the small beaches, because the baths at the Oatley Pleasure Grounds are unsafe. A shark could get in there any time." He said, "that if the baths were repaired people would swim there instead of from unprotected beaches."

++++

Friday the 14th of January 1944 A young lad became the first shark attack victim of the season, Peter Wier lost his right leg, and his left leg was severely lacerated. Peter, who was on holidays was surfing a few feet from the shore at First Beach, Forster, on the North Coast of Sydney in the afternoon, when the shark attacked. It grabbed his leg, and he screamed for help and bashed at the water with his hands. The shark released him but made a second attack before other surfers could reach him. They dragged him to the beach, and he was later taken to the hospital and had his right leg amputated.

++++

Tuesday, October 1935

A narrow escape occurred in the afternoon near Ramsgate, Botany Bay when a mother and her child had narrowly escaped a shark. About forty public works employees who were at work in the vicinity were horrified when they saw a shark chasing the two from the water, but they were too far away to be in a position to render assistance.

The mother and her child, a girl aged about seven, were paddling in about two feet of water several yards from the beach about 220 yards from the Ramsgate Baths when the cry of 'Shark' went up. The workmen had seen the shark cruising around during the day and were on the lookout. Recognizing the danger in a flash, the mother seized her little girl, and together they dashed through the small breakers with the shark in hot pursuit.

The shark gained on them quickly, but the workmen declared that they beat it to the shore just in time by a couple of yards, It made such a vicious snap at them as they left the water, that it leaped right on to the dry sand and lay stranded on the beach. Some of the men said later that the shark tried for three minutes to regain its position in the water and succeeded only when a breaker more significant than the rest broke over it as there was just enough water for the monster to turn around quickly and disappear into the bay.

++++

Thursday 4th February 1937

A shark tore a large hole In a 16-foot launch in Botany Bay, and swam, near the vessel after it had partly submerged. The occupants remained kneeling in the boat with water up to their necks for four hours hoping to be rescued sooner than later. They were Albert Cree aged 54, and John Blacksall, 72 who joined Cree for a day of fishing, But a day they would never forget, The vessel left Botany Bay before dawn, about 3 am in the morning. The Heads had almost been reached when the two men heard a big swishing sound but it was too dark to see what it could be. Suddenly a shark was biting through the hull.

They were utterly exhausted when rescued from their perilous position three miles outside of the Heads, shortly after 7 am. Several teeth, from the shark, were embedded in the half-inch planks of the hull from when it attacked their vessel, and it was towed to shore.

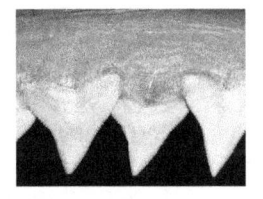

++++

Wallace John McCutcheon aged 15 years, escaped death by a very narrow margin when he was attacked by a 10-foot shark in the George's River at East Hills. The monster's teeth missing his heart by only half an inch. The boy showed great fortitude and although terribly injured, was recovering well.

++++

Shark Attack

An exceedingly sad accident occurred at Cape St. George Lighthouse, Jervis Bay, on Sunday the 17th of November 1895. Mr Edward Bailey, the first assistant keeper, took two of his sons, aged ten years and six years, to fish off a ledge of rocks a little distance away from the lighthouse. Suddenly a huge wave washed over the shelf of rocks and carried Mr Bailey into the sea. He started to swim back to the ledge, but when about half way he turned on his back to float, apparently with the view to recover his breath. While his young sons watched in horror, he suddenly disappeared feet first, being evidently taken down by a shark, three of these monsters had been seen swimming near the spot a few moments previously.

++++

At Strand Beach, near Kissing Point, Townsville, Queensland, the scene of a horrific shark accident occurred late in the afternoon on Wednesday the 4th January 1933.
Stanley Victor Locksley aged 38 years, a shearing cook, of the Hughenden Station, was shockingly mutilated when he was bathing in shallow water by a giant Grey shark. He died almost immediately.
Stanley, with Frederick Pianta, 14 went to the beach to bathe. While both were sitting down in three feet of water,
young Frederick saw a Grey form appear, and he hurriedly left the water, calling to his friend to make haste. When he reached the water's edge, the lad looked around and saw Stanley struggling

on his knees and the water all about him was reddened with blood. The shark was then swimming away. Rushing to the spot, Frederick found Stanley dead and torn almost in halves, as the shark's first rush was so fast and the attack so severe that the victim had no time to utter a cry.

A couple weeks earlier a resident with his dog was leaving the water at the same spot, and the dog was snapped in halves by a giant shark which had rushed into the shallow water.

++++

In the later months of 1965, the late Sir Victor Coppleson investigated many shark attacks and found no correlation between attacks and weather, tide or turbidity. Many attacks have taken place on the shore ward side of sand bars. Frequently they occur in waist-deep water and within 50 yards of shore. Attacks have been made on bathers inshore from other bathers.

++++

Kingston, was full of intense excitement during the week of December 26th 1905, when an enormous shark which has been haunting the local waters for the last week. Due to a regatta being held on Saturday. There have been strenuous efforts being made to capture the monster. Twice the shark had hooks that were embedded into its skin but he succeeded in tearing them away. Yesterday a band of men went to the jetty armed with explosives, but no shark met the appointment time. The monster of the deep was estimated to measure approx 18 feet.

++++

The Grey Nurse Shark

The Grey Nurse (Carcharias Taurus) also known as the sand tiger or spotted ragged tooth shark, prefer shallow sandy bottoms, inshore, and or gutters and rock caves or rocky reefs around islands. Generally, the Grey Nurse is not aggressive but can be dangerous if provoked or it feels cornered. Their teeth, designed for holding its food more than cutting the food. They can grow to about 3.2 meters in length and are thought to live for approx 30 - 40 years.

The Grey Nurse is nocturnal; they are generally inactive during the day. They tend to gather in groups of up to 40 nurse's during the day and hunt alone at night.

The east coast Grey Nurse sharks are listed as Critically endangered while the west coast ones are listed as vulnerable. Many shark attacks had been incorrectly blamed on the Grey-nurse which lead to indiscriminate killing of the species. The species has a large, stout Grey body.

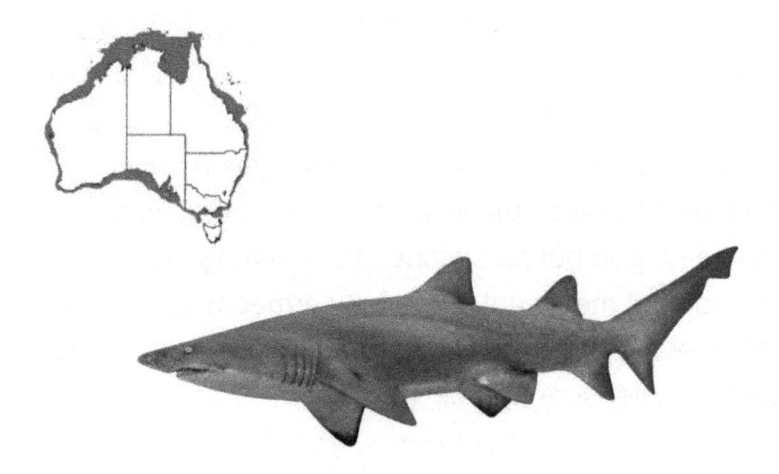

Sharks Attack

The Bull Shark

The Bull shark (Carcharhinus Leucas) also is known as many other names like the River Shark, Freshwater Whaler and the Estuary Whaler.

Bull Sharks can live in a variety of habitats from coastal marine waters, estuaries to freshwater in river systems. Their diet is omnivorous which includes fish, including other sharks, dolphins, turtles, birds but it can also consist of terrestrial mammals like antelope, cattle, people, dogs etc.

The shark is an aggressive species and is considered dangerous to humans. The species is found in murky water along the east coast of Australia, where splashing from a swimmer could be easy prey.

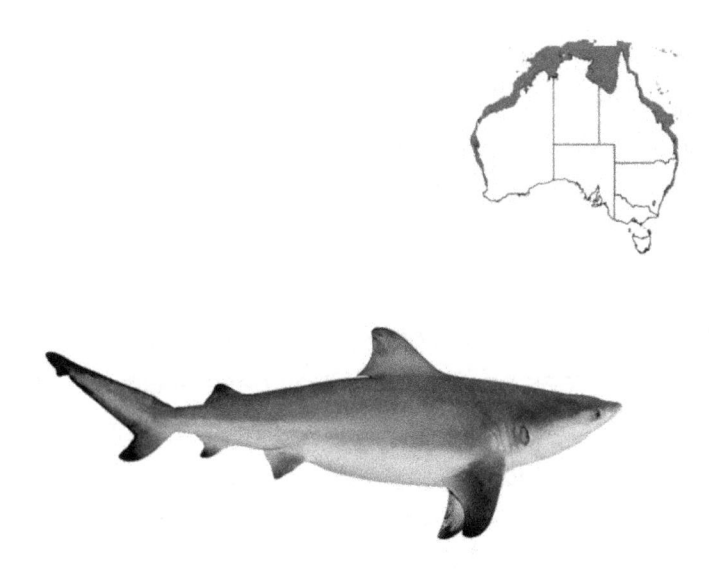

Man v Shark

As humans, we assume we have the right to use or take anything we want in the world, and the ocean is one of those places.
We hear people say sharks are sick; there has to be something wrong with it if they have attacked someone. And yet humans attack, pick on, abuse, put down, disrespect everyone and anything all the time. Who is the sicker?

But all a shark is doing is just being natural and doing what comes naturally to them.
Sharks aren't sick at all, and yes shark attacks occur, but shark culling does not work. Let's say a shark has attacked someone; it's not like the authorities can get a group of sharks together and make them do a line up to pick out the rotten fish. If they do a shark cull, there is no proof that they would have caught the shark that has done the attack or a shark that has now, discovered the taste of human blood.

Killing off sharks is not the answer. Do the authorities kill off people who hurt other people, in some places in the world, yes. But in other areas no, because they believe life is valuable. Well why are sharks any different, they are an essential part of the ocean, and without them, all the dead fish would decay, and the sea would turn putrid. If we kill off one crucial part of the food chain, the rest will collapse.

Some councils along the coast, where plenty of people flock to beaches have tried drum-lines and baited the area or added nets to prevent sharks from entering coastal swimming areas, but either the netting doesn't go high enough, or they have large holes in them where sharks can swim straight through.
The only true way one can reduce shark attacks is to educate humans on safety when going swimming or any other activity at the beach.

Our thinking, our mindset has to change!
Just like someone on Ice, who goes crazy, high as a kite, so do sharks; on blood, they lose their minds, and their mouth goes into a biting frenzy reaction and their brain kicks in thinking, "Oh my god, I gotta have that whether it is animal or human.
Everything is fine until there is blood.

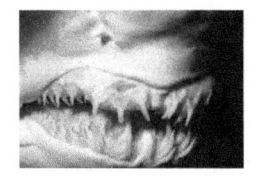

++++

Surviving a shark attack

You've gone to the beach, you have put your bag, towel, and other gear down on the sand and walked down to the water's edge, stepping in just slightly while lifting your jeans pants leg, tapping at the water to see if it was warm, refreshing etc.
This tapping sends out vibrations into the water, like knocking at the door to a home. But this home is different; it is the home to the non-walking kind. They live out their lives in peace and harmony, and then they die depending on each one's life-cycle, some gobble at their food while others like sharks have teeth for chomping down on a range of foods.
You walk back to your gear on the beach and sit down, and then proceed to open up and consume your packet of fish and chips while watching others in the water having fun splashing around in the surf.

You decide that you have had enough eating and you walk back into the water and decide to lean forward into a slight dive position to get wet all at once and dive straight into the waves that are now forming although you still have sticky fishy fingers from eating your fish and chips.
Everything is fine you have been swimming around for some time like any other day you have gone to the beach before, doing the same thing. But this time seems different; you have swum out a little deeper, and you feel something is watching you.

So you turn to head back to the shore, and you see a shark's fin out of the corner of your eye, closing in on you. Then you remember the fish and chips you had just consumed on the beach. Your salt content in your body would be extremely high and just by being in the water your bodies fluid is flowing out into the sea from your nose, mouth and other places giving the shark a taste of you even before it has bitten you. What should you try?

1) The number one thing, one must do to survive a shark attack is to get out of the water; quickly but calmly without putting anyone else into danger.
2) If you can't get out of the water in time, you need to stay calm; you will need your wits about you, to be able to get to the shore safely.
3) If the shark is close and it can't see what you are going to do, try hitting the top of its nose, making sure you won't miss and having your hand go into its mouth. But make sure you bump it, on the top side of its snout because if you are hitting it, under the nose, this will trigger the mouth to open as it is like a trigger reaction the mouth will begin automatically. Hopefully, this could give you enough time to get out of the water!
4) If the shark has you in its teeth, don't play dead, you have to fight, fight and keep fighting if you want to survive a shark attack. without moving your body too much as this movement along with

Surviving

the shark's teeth will cut into you more. Just hitting the shark on its back won't do much at all. You have to attack its eyes and gills, get your fingers in there, to get the shark to release you and then get out of the water as quickly as possible.

So tips to remember
1) Don't freeze up!
2) Fight, Fight and keep Fighting
3) Attack the Eyes and Gills
4) Don't swim away in a panic; you will look like easy prey, and you need to keep an eye on where the shark is at all times.
5) Don't give up!

And if you survive the attack, you still need to survive the trip to the hospital, where you may be able to live to tell your tale.

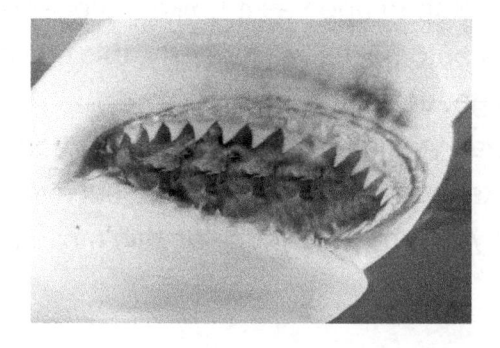

Great white Shark

The Great White Shark (Carcharodon carcharias) also known as White Sharks, White Pointer and Great White. These magnificent fish grow to lengths for Female: 4.5 – 6.4 m (Adult), Male: 3.5 – 4 m (Adult) and can weigh as much as 3000 kg. The Great White Shark can live for about 30 - 40 years, can feed on large prey and a single Great White consumes about 11 tons of food in a year. White Shark meat is not recommended for human consumption, mainly because it has a very high mercury level in its flesh.
These carnivores mostly eat dolphins, seals, some jelly fish, fish, other sharks and the occasional human but they prefer a more fatty meal than feeding on some skinny slow moving protein meal. They also like the occasionally sea turtle.